Toxic Maternal

C. A. Baynam

*To Stuart
Thank you So Much
For your Support
Your amazing
CABaynam.*

Copyright © 2023 by C.A. Baynam

All rights reserved.

No portion of this book may be reproduced in any form without written permission from
the publisher or author,
except as permitted by UK copyright law.
Cover Design by Christy Aldridge
Editors Amanda Jean Ruzsa & Sidney Shiv

Blurbs

"Not since Jack Ketchum's 'A Girl Next Door' has a story shaken me to my very core the way this one has.
Toxic Maternal is brutal, unforgiving, and yet beautifully heartbreaking." -Stuart Bray (Author of Violence on the Meek)
"This story is brutally sexual, disgustingly violent, and full of gore you can taste and feel.
In other words... it's everything splatterpunk should be."
-Chisto Healy (Author of The Gateway in Apartment 8)
"Toxic Maternal is a raw look into the depraved.
Baynam keeps the reader biting their nails with each page and wanting more!" -Chuck Nasty (Author of Thirsy)
C. A. Baynam delivers a suckerpunch of extreme proportions with 'Toxic Maternal'.
Her ability to craft the monsters, even the ones we grew up with, is a thing of horrific beauty.
Deranged, disgusting, and delicious, this book is a must for your satanic selves to gorge on." -Elton Skelter, author of 'Monomania'
"A chillingly epic tale of an overbearing Mother consumed by her unconditional dark desires. It's uncomfortable.
It pushes the boundaries of your mind, compelling you to read on and on. C.A. Baynam's creation is a thing nightmares are made of.
The central question arises: can anyone escape the clutches of the

house that Mother created, or will they be trapped forever in its menacing embrace?"

- Dan Shrader, author of Those Who Live in Darkness: Volume One

TRIGGER WARNINGS

This book contains scenes of a graphic nature
Incest, Sexual Abuse, Cannibalism, and Infant Death.
There may be a couple of others that are not mentioned here.

To my amazing other half, Glyn.
Love you with all my heart even though you are as crazy as me,
and
To my kids, who put up with my crazy, because they have to.

Contents

1. Prologue   1
2. Chapter One   3
3. Chapter Two   6
4. Chapter Three   11
5. Chapter Four   14
6. Chapter Five   17
7. Chapter Six   19
8. Chapter Seven   21
9. Chapter Eight   23
10. Chapter Nine   25
11. Chapter Ten   28
12. Chapter Eleven   29
13. Chapter Twelve   30
14. Chapter Thirteen   33
15. Chapter Fourteen   35
16. Chapter Fifteen   38
17. Chapter Sixteen   41
18. Chapter Seventeen   44

Acknowledgements	46
More by C.A. Baynam	47

Prologue

She sat at the dining table like any other morning. A steaming hot bowl of tasteless gloop sat before her, steam rising and misting her glasses. Shakily, she wiped the condensation away with her sleeve.

Picking up her spoon, she watched as Andrew walked into the room. His sweater was stretched over his hands, preventing the hot porcelain bowl from burning his skin.

"Sit the fuck down now!" his mother shrieked at him.

The very sound of her voice sent shivers down their spines. Goosebumps raised on their skin as if their bodies already knew what was about to happen.

Mother gave them both an icy glare that pierced their very souls; there was no love, no remorse, just a black heart.

"And what do you think you're looking at cunt?" Mother's attention now turned to Sarah, droplets of spit landing at the side of the bowl.

Mother calmly walked over to the table. A sinister smile appeared across her face.

Sarah could sense her mother's presence lurking behind her and felt sharp fingernails digging into the back of her scalp. She felt the gooey porridge burn through her skin as her face slammed into her bowl. The bowl sliced through her eyebrow and forehead as it broke.

Porridge and blood mixed together and dropped to the floor as Sarah slid from the wooden chair.

Andrew sat in silence, sobbing.

Sarah sat up, her hand putting pressure on her wound. She screamed as she felt a new influx of pain shoot through her fingers and up her arm, as her mother stomped on her fingers.

Falling to the ground, Mother grabbed her hair again, tugging her across the kitchen floor.

"No, Mommy, no, please don't."

Sarah heard a door creak open, each muscle in her body tightening. She tried to push back as she was forced through the door by Mother's foot.

Sarah tumbled down the dusty basement stairs, smashing her elbow on the last wooden step as she hit the floor.

Fear rocked her body as she watched the door close at the top of the stairs, plunging her into darkness.

"Mommmmmy."

Chapter One

The mansion stood as a haunting relic of their childhood, nestled amidst an overgrown landscape that whispered untold secrets. The once-grand structure, now weathered and weary, bore the scars of decades under the relentless assault of nature and neglect. Its decaying facade, cracked and peeling, seemed to writhe in the moonlight as if the very essence of the building recoiled from the touch of time.

The full moon hung in the ink-black sky like a watchful eye, casting an eery glow upon the mansion grounds. The gnarled branches of ancient trees stretched like skeletal fingers. Their shadows danced in grotesque patterns on the mansion's crumbling walls.

Windows, cracked and half-boarded, stared out like vacant eyes from the darkness within. Faint, flickering lights danced in the depths of the mansion, casting ominous shadows that seemed to play tricks on the mind.

"I don't get why we must come back here every goddamn fucking full moon, Andy. I've never understood her stupid fucking rule. I hate her, and I hate this place." Sarah stared out the car window, tears sliding down her rosy red cheeks. Her mind raced in all directions, anger filling her veins. Her long blonde hair danced around her face from the cold breeze.

Turning, he looked at his sister. Sarah turned to face him. he gave her a heartfelt smile to reassure her that everything would be alright. But in reality, Andrew knew it wasn't. Going home filled him with fear. His eyes drifted to the faded scar on Sarah's face, running down the side of her forehead through her eyebrow. Andrew felt sick to his stomach, remembering that day—one of Mother's many tantrums.

As the car pulled onto the driveway, dread filled his body. Andrew hated this place. The hairs on his arms began to rise, and goosebumps covered his body. The sight of home, if he could even call it that, sent shivers down his spine.

He shook himself, trying to clear his mind of the shit they both had to endure as children. It was hard for them both to return to this place—their childhood home. But what terrified them both most of all was coming back to her.

Andrew never understood why they had to come back every full moon. It had always been a mystery to them both.

He was married to his beautiful wife, Anna. She had been a beacon in his darkness; they had made a family together.

Sarah had finally moved on with her life. She was finally happy.

Both had successful careers, with no help from their mother. They had left this place behind them.

Sarah and Andrew dreaded the phone ringing, seeing their mother's name on the screen. No politeness, just a vile, sickening, crackling order.

"HOME NOW!!"

"You know it's not that easy, Andy. Look what she did last time I said I wasn't coming. She had her mates from the sheriff's station come and arrest me. They dragged me here in fucking handcuffs. I almost lost my job because of her. There's no saying no. The only time you and I will ever be free is when she's dead."

Andrew felt the heat from her breath as she spoke, her anger filling the confined space of the car. He pulled the car into the driveway and switched off the engine. His heart was beating so fast. It almost felt like it was beating out of his chest. Beads of sweat trickled down his forehead as he looked at the house. Opening the car door, the wind whistled around him. He welcomed the cold air on his skin.

He looked up at the window where his bedroom used to be. Not even having to step one foot inside the house, he knew the inside looked completely the same like the house itself was stuck in time, waiting for those innocent little children to come back and play.

Walking around to the back of the car, he opened the boot and grabbed their suitcases.

Having built up her courage to get out of the car, Sarah waited nervously and smiled.

"It will all be okay. We'll get these couple of days over and done with, and next time, we'll tell her to fuck off," Andrew said.

"The only time you and I will ever be free is when she's dead," Sarah repeated to her brother. She used her sleeve to wipe away her tears.

He nodded in understanding. She was right. He watched her as she took a deep breath and composed herself.

This would never end. It was either mother's way or no way at all.

—·—

Chapter Two

"Well, you both took your fucking time getting here." Mother appeared in the doorway, glaring down at them as they neared the stairs. Her long, mahogany hair blew around her face in the wind. "You should have been here the minute the moon started to rise. You've no fucking excuses. Now get in the house."

Her coldness sent shivers down their spines. Andrew and Sarah looked at each other with fear in their eyes, bewildered. They hadn't even stepped inside the house, and she was already screaming at them.

Sarah turned, grabbing the car door handle. Her body was trembling.

"It will be okay. This is the last time, Sarah. We'll figure something out before the next full moon." Andrew took her hand in his.

She looked at him and nodded her head in agreement. "The last time."

Begrudgingly, they grabbed their suitcases and slowly made their way up the dusty stairs to the front door, the musty odour stinging their noses the closer they got—the all-too-familiar smell of their unhappy childhoods.

Sarah made her way up the floral carpeted staircase to her bedroom, her hand gliding up the ice-cold metal bannister.

Andrew followed her, standing by his bedroom door, listening to his mother's voice. She had visitors. Her pretence of being nice was sickening. He couldn't remember a time when she had ever been nice to him or Sarah.

He giggled as he listened to his mother trying to cosy up to someone. A male. *Maybe if she's getting some dick, she'll be more pleasant to be around.* He laughed to himself, choking down bile at the same time. In reality, he knew that would never happen.

Kicking his suitcase under his bed, he glanced over at Sarah. She was carefully folding her clothes and placing them in the dresser drawers.

Her bed was freshly made, with the same bedding she had as a child—pink teddy bears. The pattern had faded over the years. But the bed restraints still hung to the floor.

"Get in bed, Sarah," Mother snarled.

Sarah jumped in fright at the sound of Mother's voice. She could smell the Channel No.5 that Mother was wearing. The scent overpowered her nostrils. "Mother, I'm not a child anymore. You can't treat me like this. I will not be made to go to bed. I will go when I want to and will most certainly not be strapped down." Shaking, Sarah stood her ground, waving her finger at her mother. Sarah couldn't move. Her feet felt as if the ground had swallowed them. Even through the fear, she dared to smile.

Mother stormed out of the room and nearly ran down the stairs.

Andrew looked at Sarah from his room worriedly. She was smiling. It felt a little like a small triumph.

Sarah could hear her mother's hushed voice as she shut the bedroom door. For once, she felt proud of herself. She had finally stood up to the woman. She undressed, leaving her panties on, and neatly folded the rest, then placed them on the stool.

As she pulled the sheets back on the bed, her mother burst through the door.

"You think you're going to chat me, you little whore?" Mother lurched at Sarah.

Sarah felt the sting of Mother's slap across her face. Five red welts rose across her cheek as her skin burned and swelled. She fell backwards from the force against the side of the bed, pain shooting through her back as she slid down onto the floor.

"Get her up," her mother commanded.

Dazed, Sarah looked up to see two young men running over to her. Fear raced through her. As she scrambled to get up, her mother kicked her feet out from under her. Pain shook through her spine as she landed hard on the wooden floor.

The men grabbed her, one on either side, hauling her off the floor. They forced her down on the bed. Sarah screamed at the top of her lungs, kicking out at them. Her mother grabbed her ankles and squeezed with all of her strength. Sarah's screams reached a new height as she felt Mother's nails dig into her flesh. Blood trickled onto the bed sheets.

Sarah gave up and lay completely still. As she stared at the ceiling, she knew her struggle was futile. Her cheek stung as the tears rolled over the swollen finger marks.

She felt the men's rough hands on her skin as they fastened the restraints tightly around each wrist. They glided their hands between her legs teasingly as they fastened her ankles at the bottom of the bed.

Leaving the room, they glance back at a semi-nude Sarah, each eyeing her exposed breasts, giggling to themselves.

Mother sat on the edge of the bed and smiled at her. "Why do you make things so difficult, Sarah? Look at the mess you've made. You can stay in here all day tomorrow to reflect on what you've done here tonight." She looked at the bloodstained sheets. She pressed a finger to a droplet of blood, then brought it to her mouth and licked her finger.

Sarah looked out of the barred window. Her face was wet with tears. She felt her mother's cold, clammy hand on her thigh. The hand slowly slid up towards her groin.

Mother cupped Sarah's privates, squeezing tightly. Sarah let out a sharp cry as she felt her mother's nails dig into her skin. Mother's fingers shoved the soft, lacy fabric of Sarah's panties to one side and slid a finger into her vagina. Her long fingernail scratched Sarah as it went deep inside.

Sarah, feeling revolted, tried pushing her mother away, but the straps were so tight she couldn't move her hands or feet. She wanted to throw up as she felt her mother slide in another finger. She felt them rooting within—moving, scratching.

"You were told to be on time today." Mother slid another finger inside.

"Mom, please stop," Sarah screamed in discomfort. Her long brown hair clung across her wet face.

Mother slowly removed her fingers, gliding her wet digits up Sarah's belly. She turned to face her as she moved, quickly grabbing Sarah's exposed nipples between her fingers. "You always defy me, Sarah. It's a simple rule. If you want to live away from the house, you must return every full moon. On time. And whilst in my house, you live by my rules. Or you face the consequences."

Getting up from the bed, she roughly twisted Sarah's nipples. She listened gleefully as Sarah squealed, begging her to let go. "You will stay like this 'til moonrise tomorrow. And you will behave, Sarah." She walked out of the room, leaving the door wide open, her daughter's nakedness on full display.

Sarah's pleading screams echoed in her mother's ears as she walked down the hallway.

CHAPTER THREE

Andrew had already been restrained. He saw Mother flying back up the stairs to confront Sarah, closely followed by a few men. Two went into Sarah's room, and the other two pushed him back into his room. He wasn't going to fight them; Andrew already knew he'd lost this fight. He could see something was very wrong this time coming home.

Lying on the bed, naked, he had heard his mother talking to Sarah. He lay there, wishing he'd never brought her back to this place. Sarah had been right.

They should never have come.

Mother opened his door. "Elizabeth will be up in a moment. You need to give her some of that baby juice you have," she said, pointing at his penis. Smiling, she turned her back to him.

"Fuck you, no. I'm fucking married," he screamed.

Mother almost sang as she walked down the stairs, "You'll do as I say, Andrew, or I'll ask Chris to come and see to that whore you call a sister."

Andrew lay there in the dark, listening to Sarah sobbing. He thought about Anna and his children. He wished he was at home with them now. Andrew could almost smell the freshly baked cookies that

Anna said she would make. Their sweet, sugary taste made his tongue tingle when he thought about them.

Mother was downstairs. The two men were with her, and there were other hushed voices. He'd never thought the house was this busy before. He was confused.

There was a creaking noise.

Then another.

Someone was walking up the stairs.

Andrew looked at the doorway as a naked figure walked into his room. Her face was shrouded in a black veil. She walked closer to the bed and touched his feet.

"Go away," Andrew shouted. He could see her a little clearer now. Although the veil covered most of her face, he glimpsed a peek as she climbed onto the bed. She had a stubbled chin, like a man who hadn't shaved in a day or two. He felt the bed dip with her weight as she knelt on all fours over his body.

The rolls of her flesh buried his toes. Vomit rose in his throat.

The woman crawled slowly up his body, her head bending down to his crotch. He could feel her hot breath on his skin. Her tongue licked his sack, dragging the loose skin upwards. Her saliva ran down between his butt cheeks.

Andrew turned his head and threw up over his pillow.

She giggled as she ran her tongue around the tip of his shaft, taking it in her mouth, sucking him like a lollipop. The stubble pricked his balls as his shaft disappeared deep into her mouth.

"Stop," Andrew cried out. He could feel his blood pulsating in his penis as he unwillingly grew hard. He tried to push this beast of a woman off his body. She crawled further up the bed, hovered above him, skillfully placed his penis between her fat rolls, and tucked it inside her. Andrew felt the warmth of her vagina around his shaft as she rode him.

Eventually, he ejaculated inside her. Along with it, a wave of disbelief and disgust engulfed him. He couldn't believe Mother made this happen. The woman silenced his thoughts, still sitting on his cock, laughing. She bent down, licking vomit from his cheek, slowly bringing her tongue down to his neck. Andrew felt a surge of pain as her teeth dug into his skin.

He screamed.

Mother appeared at the doorway, a sinister smile on her face. "Now, now, Elizabeth," she said as she helped her off the bed.

"I just wanted a quick taste, mother."

"Go and get yourself cleaned up."

"I hate you," Andrew cried, his neck feeling like he had been stabbed with a hot poker, blood oozing from the bites on his neck and shoulder. "You're no fucking mother. You're a lonely old hag. You don't know how to be a..."

"Elizabeth was dumped on the doorstep when she was five." Mother stood in the doorway. "Always managed to keep the children I despise away from the children I should rightly have—the ones who care more about their mother than her own wretched blood. You two ingrates are my greatest disappointment."

Chapter Four

"Sarah has good bones, and she's ripe. She will carry very well," Mother said to the men sitting around the dining table.

"Downstairs is complete now," Chris said. "They fitted the final door last night." He leaned back in his chair, fingers interlocked behind his head.

"What do you want to do with Elizabeth's pet?"

"He'll be part of the ritual and not be allowed to interfere. I know what he's like. He'll take Sarah away the first chance he gets, and I will not allow that little cunt ever to leave this house again," Mother said in a hushed, angry voice. "He won't have the power to stop me." She looked down at her top, noticing a crinkle and straightened it.

"With what Elizabeth is doing to him anyway, he won't have the strength to even walk out of that room."

Mother got up from the chair and moved to the sink, washing her hands. "I'm going to the basement. It's time I set the last final things in motion. Bring me a little rat."

Opening the door to the basement, Mother made her way down the stairs. She pulled a cord at the bottom, and the basement glowed with an eerie light. In the depths of the old, decrepit mansion, its walls damp and slick with moisture, the air oozed an unsettling odour of decay. The uneven stone floor echoed with whispers as if the very earth held secrets.

Mother went to the table and lit the black candles. She pushed a brick jutting out of the wall, and a loud, shifting noise filled the air.

In the far back wall, a door opened to reveal a secret room. The dimly lit room had stone walls that held unusual patterns of cracked, discoloured mortar. Black and white candles, their wax melted into a ghostly glow, were scattered around the room. In the middle of the room stood an old round table. Its surface was worn with age and covered in strange carvings. Leather restraints hung from its sides.

Mother stepped over to the table, brushing her fingers lightly over it. Her fingers glided over the smooth wood finish. "Bring me the rat."

The men silently left the room.

"You will plant your seed before the moon rises tomorrow. Keep her restrained, Chris. Everything needs to go according to plan. There can be no fuck-ups, do you understand," demanded Mother.

Chris nodded a smirk on his face.

The other men came back into the room, dragging a naked man across the floor, his muffled screams barely audible behind the gag in his mouth. The men lifted him and dumped him onto the round table, his arms and legs flailing in the air as he tried to get up.

Chris closed the door.

The man looked on helplessly as the men around him began to undress. His heart pounded like a drum against his ribs. Each beat echoed the terror that clenched his chest. Sweat dripped down his forehead. Fear had taken hold of his body.

Mother stood next to the table. He watched as she slowly unbuttoned her blouse. After taking it off, she folded it neatly and set it on the table. Bending down, she removed her trousers and panties. Standing naked in front of the restrained man, she began chanting.

The 'Rat' looked at her old, wrinkled body, her skin glowing in the candlelight.

"Beneath the moon, where shadows weave," Mother screamed.

Chris and the other men gathered around the table, forming a circle. They held hands and began swaying.

"In darkness, I believe. Silent whispers, a haunting dower, embrace this being in his damnation. I am a darker power."

A subtle draft created a gentle rustle as it wove through the stillness. Mother's hair fluttered lightly as it moved past her. She picked up the black-handled athame, her knuckles turning white from the grip. The man squirmed as she climbed onto the table, straddling him like a cowgirl.

His cock stood erect as he unwillingly enjoyed the show. Mother smiled as she grabbed his cock and slid it inside her. Mother's hips move in a circular motion. She rode him hard and fast, pounding her body against his, holding the athame high above her head. She shrieked with pleasure as she brought it down, stabbing the man in the chest.

CHAPTER FIVE

The man let out a guttural scream as the blade plunged deep into his chest. As he writhed beneath her, he felt the blade move around. The searing pain surged through his body like molten lava, each pulsating wave a relentless assault on his senses. Every movement she made sent shockwaves of agony throughout his body.

His cock released its load inside her as he squirmed—a mix of pleasure, agony, and fear.

Mother lifted the knife, dripping blood on his chest. The blade gleamed in the candlelight as blood oozed from his wound onto the table. Mother looked at him, her eyes black, a strange madness on her face.

"In darkness, I believe, come to me," Mother screamed again as she went into a frenzy, plunging the knife into the man over and over. Blood flew everywhere as the blade tore through his skin.

The men's chants deafened the screams as they swayed. Unlocking hands, they turned to each other, taking one another in a loving embrace.

The man on the table could only watch as his life drained from him, forcing him to see the men kissing and touching each other as Mother rode his dying body.

The last stab of the knife drove hard into his skull. Mother rammed the blade deep, dragging it upwards and cracking his skull open like a coconut.

She lay down on his body, rubbing her breasts around in his blood. She grabbed either side of his now-exposed rib cage and pulled it apart with her bare hands. Reaching in, she grabbed the man's heart and ripped it clean from his chest cavity.

"I am the darker power," Mother screamed as she bit a chunk out of the heart. The candles began flicking, casting a soft, eerie glow on her.

Out of nowhere, a thick, ominous shadow materialised before her. The air crackled with malevolent energy as the darkness advanced towards her. Holding her breath, Mother felt the shadow draw near until it caressed her face.

A suspended moment lingered as if time itself held its breath.

The darkness continued its approach, inching closer until it almost melded with Mother. In a mysterious dance, it seemed to fuse with her very essence. Soon, the shadow enveloped her, casting a dim veil over the basement as their union unfolded.

The two entities became one in the shroud of darkness.

Chapter Six

Andrew lay there trembling, his whole body aching. The bites on his neck throbbed. He could feel the heat from them on his chin. The distinct stench of iron and copper filled the air.

He stared at the ceiling, something he had done every night as a child, waiting for his mother or one of her goons to untie him. His face wore a look of bewilderment, his cheeks wet with tears.

"What the fuck is going on?" He whispered as he heard his mother's groans and screams coming from downstairs. As a child, he had been terrified of her, and that hadn't changed with adulthood.

Just as he and Sarah had discussed last week, coming back here was indeed a mistake; he was to blame. Sarah had been adamant. She hadn't wanted to come back this time, insisting that Mother's voice was off when she spoke with her last. She had been much more worried this time. He should have listened to her; they could have hidden. Even his wife, Anna, had begged him not to go. But he knew and feared the consequences, and so did Sarah.

And so, here they were. Both were chained to their beds again, just like when they were children. He didn't dare think about what state his sister was in. He'd heard her weeping well into the night.

A tittering sound broke his thoughts at the door.

"Fuck," Andrew sighed as he turned his head to see a fat blob of skin standing on the stairs, looking straight at him.

Elizabeth glanced down the stairs as they both heard voices. Laughter echoed throughout the house, their voices getting louder as they drew nearer.

"Elizabeth," his mother's voice called out.

He smiled at Elizabeth as she stood there with a terrified look on her face.

Mother appeared next to Elizabeth on the stairs. Her skin glistened in the faint moonlight peeking in through the windows. She stood, smiling, covered head to toe in blood. Bits of flesh and guts clung to her body. Elizabeth hung her head and held her hand out in front of Mother.

"My darling girl. You want a little pet, don't you?" Mother took her hand, pulling her closer.

"I need him, Mother... I need him inside me," she smiled at Mother as they hugged on the stairs. Elizabeth couldn't resist the temptation of all that blood. She licked Mother's neck. Her tongue lightly glided along her skin, tasting the 'rat's' juices as they touched her tongue.

"You can have him." Mother smiled at her.

Elizabeth squealed and clapped her hands like an excited schoolgirl, then turned and ran up the stairs.

"But Elizabeth, you only have tonight and tomorrow. He's mine on the third night of the full moon, and I will need some of his blood to stain the table. So, you will say your goodbyes tomorrow."

Mother carried herself off into the bathroom as she heard Andrew's screams. She heard his skin tear as Elizabeth bit into his leg. "That's my girl," she laughed, closing the bathroom door.

—·—

CHAPTER SEVEN

Chris wandered up the staircase. Andrew's painful cries were blaring throughout the house. His ears were ringing. But, even still, he could hear Sarah's soft cries grow louder with each step he took. Once he reached halfway, he could see into Andrew's room. "Fuck me," he giggled to himself. He stood and watched in amusement.

Elizabeth stood at the base of the bed with the tip of Andrew's cock in her mouth. Her teeth ripped into his stretched foreskin as she tugged at him. He tried in vain to move his body in hopes of slightly alleviating the pain. The skin ripped and hung loosely in Elizabeth's mouth. Chris gagged, watching saliva run down her chin as she chewed—the flesh churning in her mouth.

"You go, baby girl, but don't be too rough with your little pet. We still need him." Chris laughed as Andrew shot him a pleading glance.

"I know, Mother told me." She spoke with a full mouth.

Andrew's face was covered in bites, his nose half gone. Blood oozed down his cheek onto the bed sheets as he continued to stare at Chris.

Mother stepped out of the bathroom naked, her body cleansed of blood. She held her hand out to Chris.

"She's done a number on him. Is he still going to be able to perform alright for the final night? The way she's going, nothing will be left of him," Chris said.

"There will be enough. Andrew's part in the ritual has already begun."

Chris looked at her, confused.

"The firstborn shall be devoured by a beast." Mother watched as Elizabeth chewed the flesh from Andrew's leg, like stripping a chicken drumstick. Blood and spit hung from her chin and dribbled onto the floor.

"Don't worry, my baby boy. You're not the first-born son. And the firstborn daughter shall bear the seed. Which you will provide for me tomorrow?" She pulled Chris closer to her.

As Andrew screamed in excruciating pain, they folded into each other's arms, a darkness surrounding them. Tenderly, Chris touched her body, holding Mother tightly. They shared a kiss that echoed the evil inside them. The shadow inside Mother began to stretch and entwine Chris, surrounding them both. It was like their dark outlines had simply melted away into a shared space. Their kiss lingered as the darkness had become a part of them both.

"You'll plant your seed tomorrow, my beautiful boy. We need them to grow. But tonight..." She unzipped his trousers, taking his throbbing cock in her hand. "Momma needs her fill." Removing her hand, she gestured for him to follow her down the hallway to her bedroom.

"You can't do this to me."

Mother laughed at Andrew's screams as she closed the bedroom door.

— • —

Chapter Eight

The following morning, Mother sat at the dining table and sipped her coffee. Andrew's screams still rang throughout the house. She raised her head to the ceiling, smiling.

"How do you know Chris's seed will be planted? I mean... how can you be sure?" A small red-headed man asked, stuffing his mouth with toast.

"For fuck's sake, Tony, how many more times have we got to explain this to you? You thick cunt!" Chris laughed.

Tony was Chris's best friend and had been for years. They did almost everything together—fuck the same girls, go hunting. Tony adored Mother and would do anything she wanted. It was Tony's job to catch the rats for Mother, and he was good at it. Every time he brought her a new one, she fucked him. Tony was in love with her.

"I've had runes carved into the walls and wood around her room. It will only be needed once. If Chris wants to play, he can. But only Chris." Mother shot Tony a stern look.

"But how do you know?"

"Tony!" Mother almost shouted through her teeth. "Do you hear those whiny screams right now?" Without a word, Tony nodded.

"Around that little bastard's room is the rune for hunger. As soon as Elizabeth steps foot through the doorway, she feels like she's starving, sexually starving." She stood and walked over to Tony, cupping his bulge in her hands. "The only thoughts on her mind right now are sex and food. Andrew is both." Mother gave his cock a pinch through his trousers.

Tony sighed.

"It has to be Chris," she turned toward Chris, pointing a finger at him. "And Tony, this time, there will be no sloppy seconds. Chris has to be the one who fucks her, no one else—no foreplay either. She doesn't deserve any kind of pleasure in her life. You leave all your playing for me, boy." She smiled as she unzipped Tony's trousers.

CHAPTER NINE

Sarah opened her eyes. They were red and puffy from crying all night, stinging from the daylight shining through the window. Her wrists were still bound to the bed. She had dark red sores and bruising from the restraints. Her wrists had swollen, making the straps tighter than they were to begin with. The insides of her thighs were sore from rubbing against her drenched panties. The bed sheets were soaked in piss. She jumped at the sight of Chris standing in the doorway, grinning at her.

"I need to go to the bathroom," she pleaded.

"Looks like you've already been, you dirty bitch. I mean, look at the state of you," Chris said gleefully. "But I guess it's fine. I've knelt in worse, and what's got to be done has to be done." Chris walked around the bed.

"*What do you want from me*? Where's Andrew?" Sarah screamed.

"Just this," Chris bent down and picked up a leather strap on the floor. He grabbed her roughly behind the knee and pulled her toward him.

"What the fuck are you doing," she cried as she tried in vain to pull her leg from his grasp.

Silently, he tugged her leg harder. She screamed as the ankle restraints cut into her skin. Chris buckled the leather strap behind her knee after ensuring it was tight. Her knee was secured to the side of the bed.

Sarah's pleading fell on deaf ears; he secured the other leg just as he did the first. She looked like a pinned-down frog on a tray, waiting to be dissected.

"Where's Andrew?" Sarah screamed as she moved her hips from side to side in an attempt to loosen the straps.

"You and I have a busy day today, sister. We're…"

"I'm not your fucking sister," Sarah spat.

Chris backhanded her across the face. "You will not interrupt me, do you understand?"

An angry red mark quickly appeared on her face as she looked at him, shocked.

"You are my sister, just not from the same dad is all. I'm the little kid that you and that dick of a brother used to tease. But enough. I'm not here for explanations and fucking chitchat." Chris pulled his trousers down and kneeled between her legs. He yanked her wet panties to one side, his cock throbbing and hard as he climbed on top of her.

Sarah felt his fingers spread her labia as he fumbled with his cock. He roughly jammed his fingers inside her, rubbing her.

"Get off me," Sarah screamed. She felt like she had been hit with a hammer as he rammed his cock inside her. She tried in vain to twist her body to throw him off, screaming louder than ever in pain as his cock penetrated her deeply.

Her forehead connected with his, and a sharp shooting pain pierced through her skull. Dazed, her head fell back against the pillow.

His hands held each side of the mattress, allowing him to keep his balance. In anger, he deliberately thrust his cock deeper inside her, his hips smacking hard against her thighs. He grunted as he released his seed, then jumped off her the moment he was done. "I'll be back," he said, mimicking Arnold Schwarzenegger from The Terminator as he pulled his trousers back on.

Sarah just lay there, looking out the window, unable to speak, crying.

"Now you're ignoring me. Seems to me you need to be grateful for your part in all this and learn some fucking manners." He walked over to the bed and grabbed her chin, squeezing hard as he turned her face to look at him. "Say thank you, Chris," he commanded, smiling.

Sarah spat at him. Her saliva landed on his cheek, and he smacked her hard across the face.

"Say thank you, Chris."

Sarah looked at him, her mouth full of blood. The defiance on her face was full of hatred. "Thank you, Chris," she whispered through her teeth.

Chris slapped her inner thigh, walked out of the room, and immediately bumped into Elizabeth. She giggled at him as she headed down the stairs. Andrew wasn't screaming anymore. Chris walked over to his room to take a look. He stood just before the doorway and brushed his fingers over the carved runes in the frame. A half-eaten finger lay at his feet.

There was blood everywhere. Bits of Andrew's flesh and muscle were discarded on the floor. Andrew weakly turned to look at Chris, his face more chewed up than it was the night before. One of his ears was gone entirely. There was a crater where his cheek should be, and flaps of flesh hung from his chin. His arms, legs, and chest all had chunks missing.

Chris shuddered. As he looked closer, he saw the rest of Andrew's foreskin had been ripped off and left lying on top of his balls.

Chapter Ten

"Defiant little bitch, dry as fuck," Chris whined as he stepped into the kitchen. Mother sat at the table, laughing as he sat down beside her. He put his hand on her thigh, opening her dressing gown with his other.

"I'll bring the other rat in in a sec," Tony muttered as he gulped his coffee.

"Yes, then the ritual will be at its full power. You'll bring Andrew down and strap him to the table." Mother smiled at Tony. "You're a good boy, Tony."

Chris's hand slid up her thigh as she spread her legs. He slid his fingers into her wet pussy and finger-fucked her, rubbing her clit with his thumb. Tony stood and walked over to them. Mother groaned as Chris's fingers delved deeper inside her. Tony bent down beside her as she rested her head against his chest. He kissed her. His tongue explored her mouth. He cupped her breasts in his hand, massaging them gently. Mother let out a satisfying scream as an orgasm enveloped her. The shadow cast an eerie glow that surrounded her.

"You'll bring her down to the basement whilst I'm dealing with the rat." She smiled at both men.

"This time tomorrow, it will all be finished." She stood and left the room.

CHAPTER ELEVEN

Mother brought the young boy in through the back door.

"Chris, sit down. I'll make you some juice."

Chris did as he was told, plonking his backside next to a young girl. The other boy sat next to the girl, and both stared at him, confused.

"You'll be nice to your brother now, do you hear me?." She pointed her finger at them.

"He's no brother of mine," the older boy mockingly said, instantly regretting it.

Mother calmly walked around the table.

"What did you say, Andrew?" She slapped the young girl across the face, knocking her to the floor.

"Mother, no," Andrew screamed. She ignored him and stomped on the young girl's fingers.

"Sarah," he screamed, tears running down his cheeks. He had to sit there and watch his mother beat up his baby sister. He turned to Chris, pleading with him to help her, as Mother dragged Sarah up from the floor and pushed her onto a chair.

"You'll not move all day, Sarah. You can thank your brother Andrew for that."

Chris only laughed.

CHAPTER TWELVE

Tony reached into the cage. He removed the padlock from the cage and shoved it into his pocket.

The woman on the end of the chain kicked at him as he dragged her to the carved table.

"What the fuck's going on?" She screamed and punched Tony hard, catching his manly jewels. He fell to the ground, letting go of the chain. She made a run for the basement steps. As she reached the top, Chris, who had overheard the commotion, waited at the doorway and elbowed her in the face as she came around the corner. He grabbed the chain and dragged the screaming woman back down to the basement.

"Fucking twat, can't you take a pussy slap to the balls?"

"Weren't no pussy slap Chris, fucking bitch." Tony slammed her down on the table. "Keep fucking still, or I'll snap your neck in two."

Tony pulled the neck chain high above her head as Chris strapped her arms and legs down. Mother walked in just as they finished securing the woman. Three other men followed her. Chris and Tony removed their clothes and got into position.

One stood at the rat's head, the other at her feet.

"Shhh shhh shhh, it's only going to hurt a little, little rat," Chris taunted the woman.

Mother wasted no time mounting the woman.

Tony handed Mother a dagger. The woman's eyes widened with terror as she squirmed between Mother's legs. Mother clenched her thighs, squeezing the woman tightly, making her scream.

"Screaming, to me, dear, is like music. A sweet, chilling lullaby to help me drift off to sleep." Mother laughed as Chris stabbed needles into both of the woman's ears. Her screams took on a higher pitch.

"Hear the birth of a star," Mother cried.

Chris held the rat's head still as Mother forced her mouth open. Sliding her fingers into her mouth, she grabbed her tongue and pulled it out as far it would go. Tears rolled down the young woman's cheeks as her mother sawed through her tongue. Gurgling noises sounded from the woman as blood trickled to the back of her throat. She thrashed around as much as she could to throw Mother off, but Mother was too strong for her.

"Speak a thousand tongues."

Mother bent to face the woman, looking her in the eyes as she pierced the right one with the blade. Clear fluid oozed out of the eye, down her cheek, mixing with the tears and blood. Mother moved to the left eye and pierced it.

"See a thousand worlds."

Mother dismounted. Her hands were sticky from the woman's blood.

"It is done. Andrew's blood now needs to mix with those in the carvings on the table, and the deal will be sealed. Finish with her," she pointed the dagger toward the woman.

"When Andrew is down here, bring Sarah to her new resting place."

"Are you killing Andrew?" Chris asked.

"Don't be stupid. That low life is beneath me. I'm not wasting any more of my time on him. His blood needs to mix. That is all. Sarah's fate will be locked. I will have my eternal power, and Elizabeth can finish her dinner while Sarah watches," she scoffed.

Mother left the room, leaving the rat in their capable hands.

— • —

Chapter Thirteen

Sarah heard her mother walking upstairs. She watched through the doorway as she came into view. Mother smiled as she saw her.

Sarah's face was swollen. Her lip was split. The sheets were yellow with piss, and a brown stain congealed near her thighs. As Mother walked past the door, she stopped for a moment.

"Not long now," she muttered.

Sarah waited until she heard her mother's bedroom door shut. She quickly unhooked her wrist from the restraint and pulled her broken thumb to one side, twisting it backwards to slide her hand through the handcuffs. She could reach the keys on the bedside table, so she snatched them up and carefully unlocked the rest.

She had no clothes. Mother had made the men remove them all. Naked, Sarah quietly walked through the door and to Andrew's room. She looked at the carvings on the doorframe, her hand brushing over them.

She turned the handle and gave the door a gentle push.

"Andrew, are you ..." her voice trailed off as she saw her brother.

The grisly vision caused her to collapse to her knees, and she placed her hand over her mouth to stifle a scream. The stench coming from the room made her gag. Her brother lay on the bed in a pool of blood. As he turned to look at her, she threw up.

His cheekbones were stripped of flesh. His nose was hanging by a string of cartilage. His fingers and toes were missing.

"I promise I'll return for you. Do you hear me?" She whispered as she leaned on the door frame to steady herself.

Turning around, Sarah slowly descended the stairs, taking one at a time. She reached for the front door as she stepped off the last step. Her body trembled with fear.

As she grasped and turned the door handle, a bolt of electricity shot through her hand straight up her arm. Sarah jolted backwards, clutching her mouth again to stop herself from screaming. The door creaked open. She walked out to the driveway.

No longer able to contain her screams, Sarah collapsed to the ground, writhing around out of sheer exhaustion and fear. She tried to stand but was roughly pulled to the ground. Her face was mashed into the gravel by an unseen foot.

"Make it stop... Make it stop!"

CHAPTER FOURTEEN

Tony moved around the table and taunted the woman. He poked, pinched and twisted her skin. With each touch, she made a gurgled cry. He looked at her bloody face and smiled as she shook her head from side to side.

"She's yours, mate. I'm gonna sit back and watch the master do his thing," Chris mocked as he grabbed his clothes from the floor.

"Fuck you, Chris. I can do the same fucked up shit you can." Tony pretended Chris hurt his feelings. He grabbed his cock in one hand and shook it in Chris's direction.

Chris laughed and sat down.

Tony walked over to a set of drawers in the corner of the room. He opened a drawer and rifled through its contents. His face lit up as his hand seemingly stroked a rusty object. He pulled it out and spun around to face Chris. "Ha, see. This has got to beat your fucked-up scale?" Tony laughed.

"Depends on what you're gonna do with it. If you're gonna stand there waving it around like an asshole, you may as well slice your dick off."

Tony stared at Chris, swinging the rusty garden shears at his side. "Why have you got to be so mean all the time?" He rubbed his eye and pretended to cry. He walked over to the table and opened the shears. "You really can be a dick sometimes."

Tony placed the woman's toes in between the blades, used both hands and pushed the blades together with all his strength. A loud cracking noise echoed through the basement as they sliced through bones, and severed toes fell to the floor. Blood pumped from the stumps and splattered on Tony's naked body. The woman's gargled screams intensified.

"Borrriiinnng," Chris sang.

Tony laughed and looked at Chris as he pretended to yawn.

"Do you want to play?" Tony, now getting annoyed with him, pointed the shears at him.

"Nope, I'll sit here and watch. You carry on. I'm interested to see where this is going to go."

Tony mounted the woman and sat on her knees. He lifted the shears and teased her by dragging them up and down her thighs. As she squirmed underneath him, excitement raced through his body, making his cock hard. He opened the shears and slid one of the blades into her vagina, sliding it in and out. When he pushed the blade deep inside her, he felt some resistance as he reached her cervix. Increasing the pressure, he pushed the blade through, into her uterus, then up into her stomach. Blood poured out of her, showering the table. She tried desperately to throw him off, bouncing him around like a Buckaroo. He closed the shears slowly, slicing through her clitoris. He stopped momentarily to look at Chris, like a child begging for a reward. He pushed the blades together and cut through her abdomen.

Throwing the shears to the floor, Tony slid his hand into her body, pulling her intestines out and dropping them onto her chest. The woman had ceased screaming. Squelching noises broke the silence as

Tony removed her liver and hurled it at Chris. "Liver and onions for tea?" Tony laughed and moved away from the table.

"That wasn't too bad, to be fair. It would have been better if she could have seen you do that," Chris jeered back at him.

Two naked men walked past them, heading toward the table.

"Fucking minions," Tony spoke through his teeth.

"Hey, at least we get to have the fun. They have to watch from the sidelines, jerking off to us while we have all the fun. Then they clean up the shit."

Chapter Fifteen

"Drag her to the bottom of the driveway and show her what happens the further she gets from this house," Mother spat at Chris. "Fucking cunt thinks she's gonna get away from me, ha. Fucking show her just how far she's gonna get."

Mother looked down at Sarah, who writhed around on the floor in agony. Her skin had turned bright red, and it looked like she was wearing a skin suit; it was pulled so tight it cracked. Blood bubbled and steamed as it spilt from the wounds. Sarah's feet and legs had blackened, slowly charred by invisible flames. Sheets of skin sloughed off her body.

Mother bent down and whispered in Sarah's ear, "Did you honestly think you could leave this house? Neither of you will, Sarah. I'd like to say you'll both die here, but *you* won't." She laughed, walked back towards the house, and left Sarah at the mercy of Chris and Tony.

"Bitch, as if I haven't got enough to do today," Chris gritted his teeth at Sarah, unclenched his fist and grabbed her by the hair before he dragged her away from the house.

"Why aren't we taking her inside?" Tony asked, confused.

"Cos we're teaching this cunt a lesson. Watch."

They dragged her further down the driveway. The rough gravel ripped her burnt skin and tore chunks of flesh away. Sarah let out a high-pitched wail as the skin began to blacken on her thighs.

"Take me back... take me back..." Sarah begged them.

"Mother said the bottom of the driveway, not far to go now." Tony laughed, absolutely mesmerised by what was happening. "It's like someone has a blow torch on her."

They took a few more steps, and spots of charred skin appeared on her back; the internal fire was eating her alive. Sarah had slipped into unconsciousness by the time they reached the end of the drive. They turned, grabbed her under both arms and dragged her almost non-existent feet behind them, along the gravel, back toward the house.

Tony looked back to see how far Sarah's body had burned. A startled look appeared on his face. "Chris," Tony patted Chris on the arm.

"What!" Chris stopped and looked at Tony. Tony could tell he was angry.

"What's going on? I ain't never seen nothing like it!" Tony almost screamed in excitement.

"Well, make the most of it. You never will again. If you're referring to her skin, yeah, I know. The closer she gets to the house, the more she'll heal. The further away from the house, her body will be a living inferno for the whole time she's away from the house," Chris angrily explained.

"So, she'll burn to death?" Tony tried to understand what he was witnessing. He glanced back again, and her thighs had healed entirely. The scrapes on her back and buttocks were gone. He watched, amazed; her skin had knit itself back together over the once-exposed bones in her feet.

"So, she'll die then? I thought she couldn't die?"

"Nope, she'll wish she had. Her body will burn, then heal slowly, bit by bit. When her body has completely healed, her skin will burn off again. A constant cycle of burning and healing. She'll be in absolute agony the whole time."

They reached the front door and threw her inside the house. Sarah, still unconscious, hit the wooden floor. There wasn't a mark on her. Her legs were completely healed.

Chris playfully punched Tony in the arm. "You don't listen, do you? Mother did go through all of this with us."

"Probably not. Can't listen to much when someone's playing with my cock."

"Tony, you're unbelievable. Mother said she wanted her to suffer for the rest of her life within the confines of this house. Mother wants to see her in pain. When Andrew's blood mixes, Sarah's life won't be worth living. She'll always be tied to Mother and this house. By the end of the night...Mother will be immortal."

They walked into the hallway, and Chris hoisted Sarah over his shoulder in a fireman's lift. They went through the kitchen and down the basement steps to Mother.

CHAPTER SIXTEEN

They made their way through the basement to the room hidden at the back. Chris passed Sarah off to one of the many naked men standing in the room. He looked at the man and pointed.

A steel cage no bigger than five feet tall was in the far corner. It was bolted to the wall. Hanging above, dangling slightly into the cage from a chain, were shackles.

The man understood Chris without exchanging words. He walked over to the cage, where he stood Sarah against the wall at the back. He used his body to hold her upright while he shackled her wrists. He left her dangling, her arms above her head, and he stepped out of the cage, then padlocked the door.

Andrew lay on the round table. His blood dripped into the wooden carvings, mingling with the blood of the rats. His body had been mauled down to the bone. The stumps where his toes and fingers should have been were now a bloody, congealed mess.

Mother stepped into the room, followed by Elizabeth, who bounced happily behind. Her giggling broke the silence. Chris held Mother's hand.

No words needed to be exchanged. The ritual had been completed the moment Andrew's body had been placed on the table. There was only one thing left for them to do.

Mother gasped as the shadow left her body and disintegrated before her eyes.

"Are you sure you want me to do this?" Chris asked.

Yes," she said, her voice stern.

Tony stood behind her as Chris picked up the dagger.

"What if..."

"Fucking do it," she screamed at him.

Chris raised the dagger and slashed it across her throat.

Mother's eyes widened, a look of shock on her face. Her hands slapped up to her throat as though she wanted to close the wound. Blood raced down her neck onto her breasts. It glided over her soft skin and dripped to the floor from her nipples. She fell backwards into Tony's arms, and he gently lowered her to the floor.

Elizabeth sat on top of Andrew. Her giggling had stopped as she stared at them, rolling skin around her mouth with her tongue.

"Chris, it didn't work. It didn't fucking work!" Tony panicked.

"Shut up, Tony." Chris's eyes welled up.

"It did..."

"Shut the fuck up, Tony," Chris bellowed at him, his gaze fixed on Mother's lifeless body on the floor.

"Good fucking riddance," Sarah spat. Then, she laughed.

Chris stared at her while anger boiled through his veins. "You think this is funny, do ya?" He laughed menacingly. He bent down and picked up the dagger. "How funny, Bitch?" He lunged at the table, grabbed a handful of Andrew's hair, and yanked his head back.

"Don't..." Sarah screamed hysterically.

But it was too late. Chris dragged the dagger across Andrew's throat.

"Think it's funny now?" He taunted her as he walked towards the cage.

"Chris," Tony muttered.

"What the fuck do you want now, Tony?" Chris whirled around, annoyed at another interruption.

"Mother!"

"Leave her be, son. She's going to suffer more than enough."

"We saw you die," Chris wore a look of confusion as he glanced at her neck—not a mark in sight. Like Sarah earlier, Mother, too, had healed. The ritual had worked; Mother was immortal.

Sarah sobbed silently. Tears rolled down her cheeks, hanging by her wrists in the cage. She glanced at Andrew and sobbed harder as Elizabeth bit a chunk of flesh from his abdomen.

CHAPTER SEVENTEEN

Sarah had lost track of time and had no idea how long it had been since the day Andrew had driven them to the house. Days and nights all mingled together. She awoke when they came into the room and turned the light on. She tried to sleep when they left her alone, turning the light off as they left.

Since she had tried to escape again, they had tightened the shackles. Her arms were left constantly raised above her head, hanging from chains bolted to the wall. The restraints were pointless. She could never leave the house; she couldn't even escape through death.

She couldn't die. She was tied to the house and Mother for eternity.

Sarah still remembered every horrific detail of Andrew's death as if it had only happened the day before. His screams as they slit his throat lingered in her ears.

In the time she had been held captive, Sarah had given birth to a beautiful baby girl. She watched as a mass of auburn hair and bright pink, bloodied skin had been pulled from her body; her newborn cry filled the silence in the basement.

Mother made Sarah watch as she stretched the umbilical cord and tightly wrapped it around the baby's neck, slowly choking her to death. Mother glared at Sarah, her eyes filled with disappointment as she ripped the placenta from her body.

Sarah sobbed and pleaded with Mother to let her hold her baby. But Mother turned away.

As the demon rose, it snatched the lifeless child out of her arms and then was gone again.

Chris visited her every night to sow his seed—an endless chore he hated; he reminded her of that every time he walked into the room.

He made jokes about the loss of their child and beat Sarah repeatedly through the long days and nights.

But the next time... The next time, it was different...

Sarah could feel it as it kicked inside her. It wasn't like before. The gradual swell of her body had taken time to grow and form.

Her stomach had swollen overnight. There was nothing gradual about it. The pain was excruciating; each kick felt like she was being sliced open from the inside.

Sarah glanced down at her stomach as the pain waves intensified. It looked like marbles rolling around beneath her skin. She screamed as her skin split open. Blood oozed down her round belly and to the floor.

The shadows stirred at the table before her as the demon appeared. A smile was plastered on his grayscale face.

A tiny hand with long talons poked through the gaping hole in Sarah's abdomen. It held one scaly arm out; it reached for its mother...

ACKNOWLEDGEMENTS

I'd like to say thank you to Stuart Bray, Chuck Nasty, and Dan Shrader, who read this book as I was writing it and being friends.
Chisto Healy and DE McMcluskey for being a remarkable critics and friends.
You all gave me the inspiration I needed to create something so sick and twisted.
Thank you to the whole Indie Horror Community for the support every one of you gives to its authors.
Love to you all.

MORE BY C.A. BAYNAM

Dark Affairs: Volume One
Dark Affairs: Volume Two
Dark Affairs: Prologue
Revenge from the Grave
The Descendants
His Undoing

Printed in Poland
by Amazon Fulfillment
Poland Sp. z o.o., Wrocław